STAR WARS®

THE POWER OF
THE DARK SIDE: BOOK 2

Adapted by Benjamin Harper

studio
A READER'S DIGEST COMPANY

White Plains, New York • Montréal, Québec • Bath, United Kingdom

Three years passed after the destruction of the Death Star,
and Darth Vader was obsessed with finding Luke Skywalker
and the rebel base. He dispatched probe droids throughout the
galaxy to search every planet for signs of the rebels' location.
When one of the droids landed on the ice planet Hoth, it sent
back images of what looked like a settlement.

"You found something?"  Darth Vader asked
Captain Piett, who was monitoring the images. The captain
showed Darth Vader the image the droid had sent. "That's
it. The rebels are there," Darth Vader confirmed. "I'm sure
Skywalker is with them. Set your course for the Hoth system!"

The rebels fought admirably against the Empire on Hoth but eventually were overtaken. They broke away from the Imperial blockade in transports by firing an ion cannon blast that temporarily knocked out the Empire's ship systems.

But the Empire managed to knock out the rebels' shield generator, allowing Darth Vader to land. He stormed into the rebel base 🔲—just in time to see the *Millennium Falcon* blast away. The rebels had escaped!

The *Millennium Falcon* escaped Hoth, but its hyperdrive engine wasn't working so it couldn't evade Imperial ships. Darth Vader ordered his troops to capture the ship no matter what.

When the *Millennium Falcon* sought refuge in an asteroid belt surrounding the planet, Piett told Darth Vader they couldn't follow because they would be destroyed by the floating rocks. "Asteroids do not concern me," Darth Vader commanded. "I want that ship, not excuses."

The Emperor contacted Darth Vader, who retreated to his private chamber. "What is thy bidding, my master?"  Darth Vader asked a holographic image of the Emperor. The Emperor told Darth Vader that they had a new enemy who was strong with the Force—Luke Skywalker.

After the Battle of Hoth, Luke had secretly flown to a swampy planet called Dagobah to train with Jedi Master Yoda and was becoming a greater threat to the Sith. Darth Vader suggested that they turn young Skywalker to the dark side of the Force. "Can it be done?" the Emperor asked. "He will join us or die, master," Darth Vader replied.

11

Growing frustrated at the Empire's lack of progress in locating the *Millennium Falcon*, Darth Vader contacted several bounty hunters and tasked them with finding the missing ship. Standing on the bridge of his Star Destroyer, Darth Vader spoke to notorious hunters Boba Fett, IG-88, Dengar, Zuckuss, 4-LOM, and Bossk. "I want them alive,"  Darth Vader commanded, especially to Boba Fett. "No disintegrations."

Admiral Piett interrupted Darth Vader to tell him that they had the *Millennium Falcon* in their sight and were about to capture the ship. But the *Falcon* evaded capture once again, escaping to Cloud City. Boba Fett tracked it there, however, and told Darth Vader of its location.

Han Solo had flown the *Millennium Falcon* to Cloud City, hoping his friend Lando Calrissian would help them repair the hyperdrive. However, thanks to Boba Fett, Darth Vader arrived ahead of Solo. Vader forced Lando to turn over Han Solo, Princess Leia, and Chewbacca—or have Cloud City taken over by the Empire. Pretending to take them for refreshments, Lando brought the unsuspecting rebels to the Sith Lord. "We would be honored if you would join us," Darth Vader said as stormtroopers flooded the room, making escape impossible.

Darth Vader set a trap so he could take Luke Skywalker to the Emperor and turn him to the dark side. Cloud City had a carbon freezing facility, but Vader wanted to test it first to make sure Luke would survive the freezing process. He ordered Han Solo to be placed in the chamber and the hero was frozen solid.

When Solo survived the procedure, Darth Vader gave him to Boba Fett, who planned to deliver him to Jabba the Hutt—a crime lord who was offering a lot of money for Han Solo's capture—on Tatooine. "Calrissian, take the princess and the Wookiee to my ship," Darth Vader then instructed Lando.

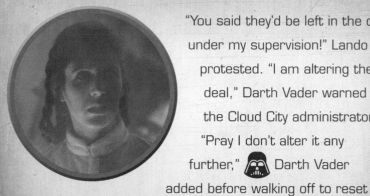

"You said they'd be left in the city under my supervision!" Lando protested. "I am altering the deal," Darth Vader warned the Cloud City administrator. "Pray I don't alter it any further," Darth Vader added before walking off to reset the trap for Luke Skywalker, who was en route to Cloud City to help his friends.

Darth Vader's plan worked. Luke Skywalker flew to Cloud City only to be lured into a fight with Darth Vader. Luke fell into the carbon freeze chamber—but managed to jump out before Vader activated the controls. Lightsabers clashing, the two fought their way throughout the center of Cloud City.

In a control room, Luke was startled by a surprise attack as Darth Vader leaped out of the shadows. Darth Vader stood back and used the Force to pummel Luke with nearby objects, eventually breaking the control room's window. Luke was cornered on a balcony.

Darth Vader fought Luke to the very edge of the balcony, which hovered above a great cavern within the center of Cloud City. As Luke struggled to keep from falling, Darth Vader declared that together they could bring order to the galaxy. "I'll never join you," Luke hissed.

"If you only knew the power of the dark side," Darth Vader taunted. "Obi-Wan never told you what happened to your father." Luke countered that during his training Obi-Wan had told him that Darth Vader had killed his father. "No, I am your father," Darth Vader said, revealing a great secret and adding, "Come with me. It is the only way."

Luke released his grip and fell away from the Dark Lord of the Sith.